WHAT HAPPENS WHEN THE MOST IMPORTANT LETTER IN THE ALPHABET GETS A BIG OWIE?

ONE OF THE OTHER LETTERS HAS TO TAKE HER PLACE WHILE SHE RECUPERATES, BUT WHO? Z IS TOO SLEEPY. AND Y ASKS TOO MANY QUESTIONS. IS O WELL-ROUNDED ENOUGH TO HANDLE THE JOB?

IT'S A REAL E-MERGENCY!

PRAISE FOR *E*-MERGENCY!

"Every page is chock-full of inventive letter-play." —*The New York Times*

★ "This artwork takes a funny story and makes it hilarious to the right readers/listeners, of which there will be many." —*School Library Journal,* starred review

★ "A nontraditional, rascally, downright hilarious alphabet book. . . . A package that readers will return to ovor and ovor. (Get it?)" —*Booklist,* starred review

★ "Comprehensive, witty entertainment from A to Z."
—*Publishers Weekly,* starred review

"Get ready to chortle. . . . The visual and print punnery will have elementary kids (and adults) guessing and laughing." —*Kirkus Reviews*

"The reading experience is hilarious. . . . There are laughs, many laughs, on every page." —*Chicago Tribune*

"Sheer madness. . . . Unceasingly witty." —*The Boston Globe*

An Indiana Young Hoosier Book Award Winner
A *Booklist* Best Book of the Year
An ALA Notable Children's Book Final Reading List selection
A Capitol Choices Final Reading List selection

THE CAST

A B C D
E F G H I
J K L M
N O P Q
R S T U
V W X Y Z
? !

THE OTHER CAST

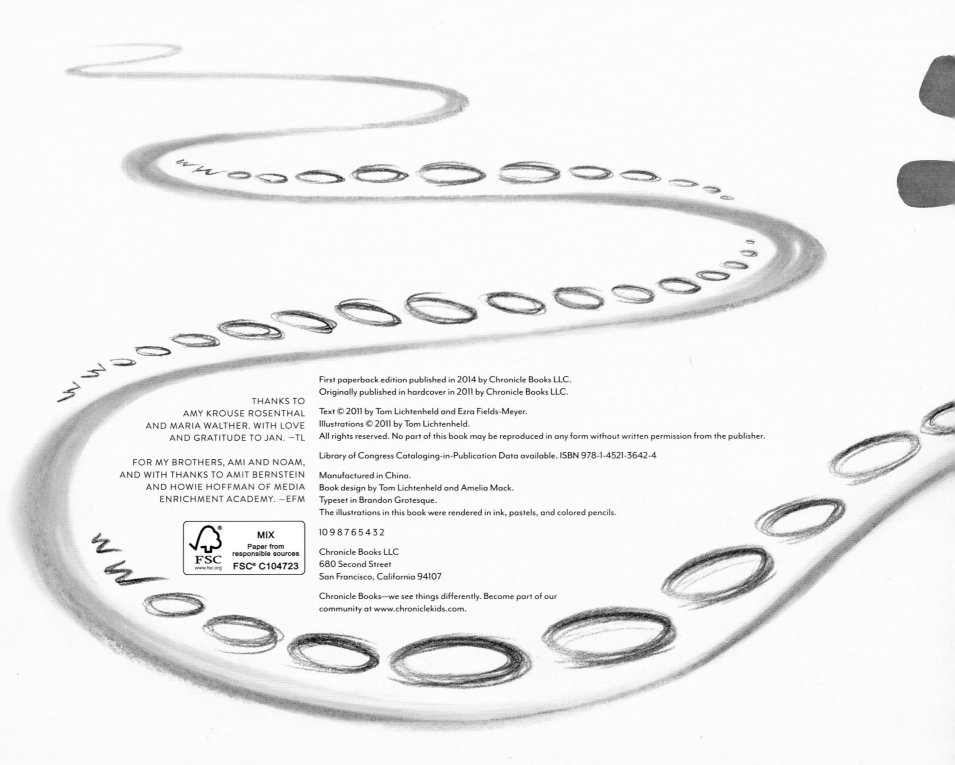

THANKS TO
AMY KROUSE ROSENTHAL
AND MARIA WALTHER. WITH LOVE
AND GRATITUDE TO JAN. —TL

FOR MY BROTHERS, AMI AND NOAM,
AND WITH THANKS TO AMIT BERNSTEIN
AND HOWIE HOFFMAN OF MEDIA
ENRICHMENT ACADEMY. —EFM

FSC MIX Paper from responsible sources FSC® C104723 www.fsc.org

First paperback edition published in 2014 by Chronicle Books LLC.
Originally published in hardcover in 2011 by Chronicle Books LLC.

Library of Congress Cataloging-in-Publication Data available. ISBN 978-1-4521-3642-4

Manufactured in China.
Book design by Tom Lichtenheld and Amelia Mack.
Typeset in Brandon Grotesque.
The illustrations in this book were rendered in ink, pastels, and colored pencils.

10 9 8 7 6 5 4 3 2

Chronicle Books LLC
680 Second Street
San Francisco, California 94107

Chronicle Books—we see things differently. Become part of our
community at www.chroniclekids.com.

E·MERGENCY!

TOM LICHTENHELD

EZRA FIELDS-MEYER

chronicle books · san francisco

ALL THE LETTERS LIVED
TOGETHER IN A BIG HOUSE.

HEY LOOK—
ALPHABET SOUP!

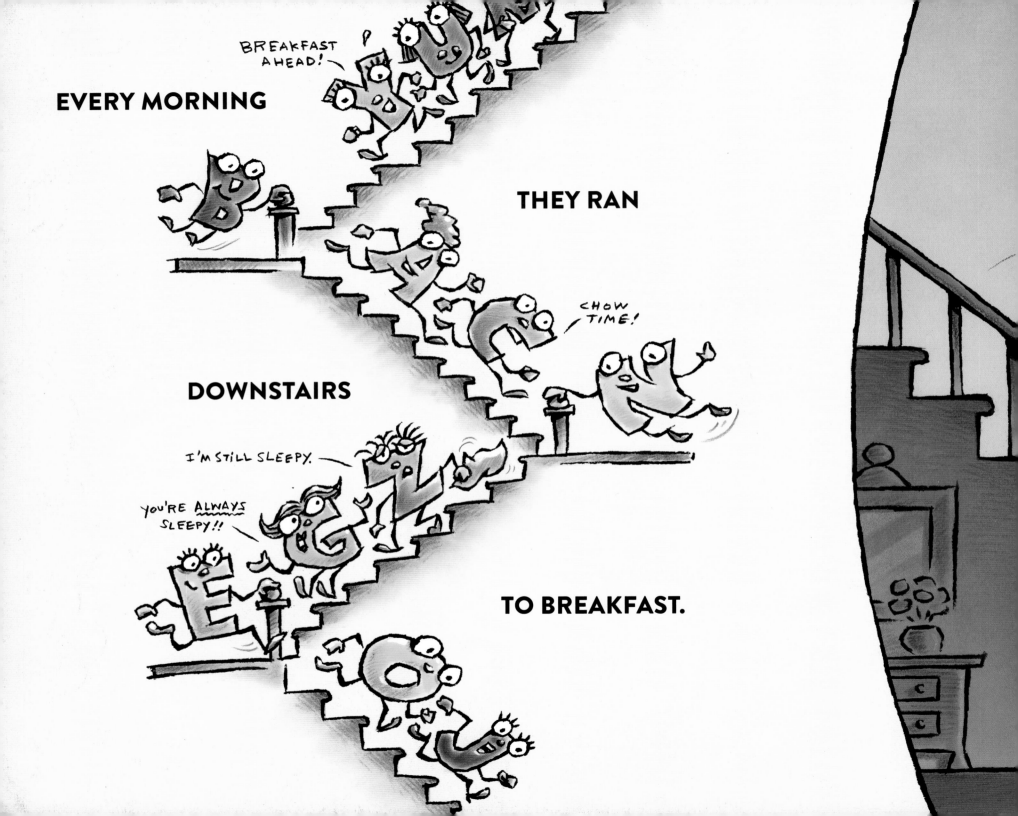

ONE MORNING, **E** CAME DOWN THE STAIRS A LITTLE TOO FAST.

THE **EMT**s RUSHED IN WITH AN **IV**, READY TO PERFORM **CPR.**

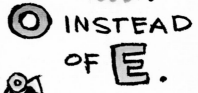

O DID HIS BEST FILLING IN FOR **E**,
BUT THE RESULTS WERE QUITE CONFUSING.

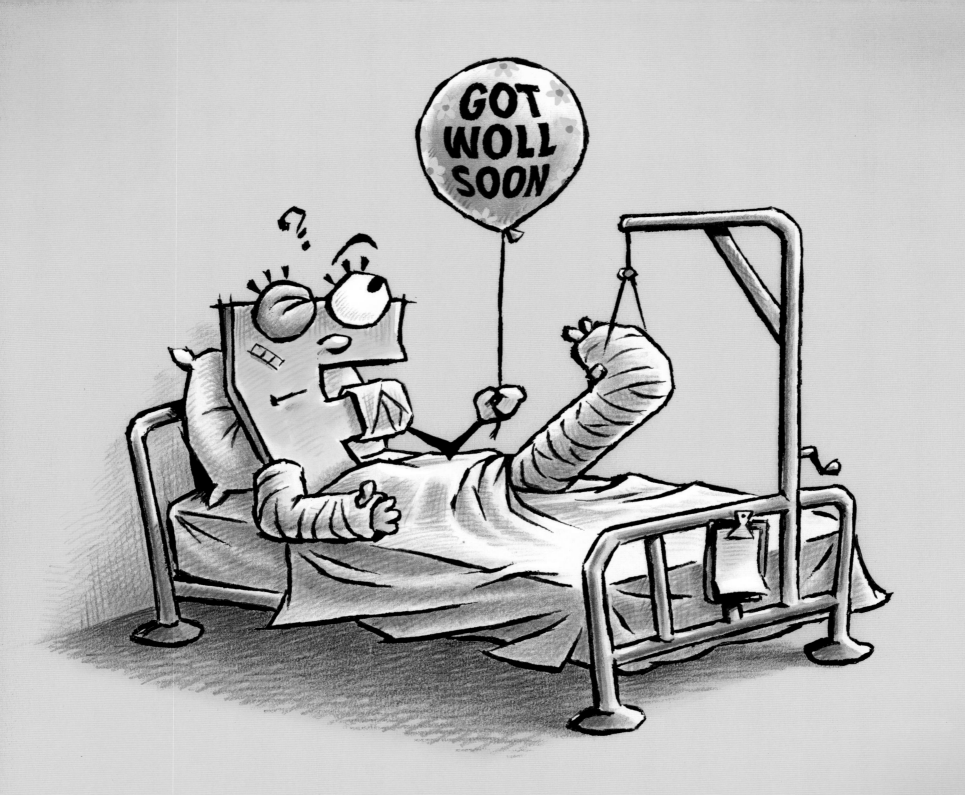

TO MAKE MATTERS WORSE, E WASN'T GETTING BETTER. THE MDs COULDN'T FIGURE OUT WHY.

A DECIDED THEY NEEDED TO TAKE A TRIP TO SPREAD THE WORD ABOUT THE LETTER.

THEY TRAVELED NEAR . . .

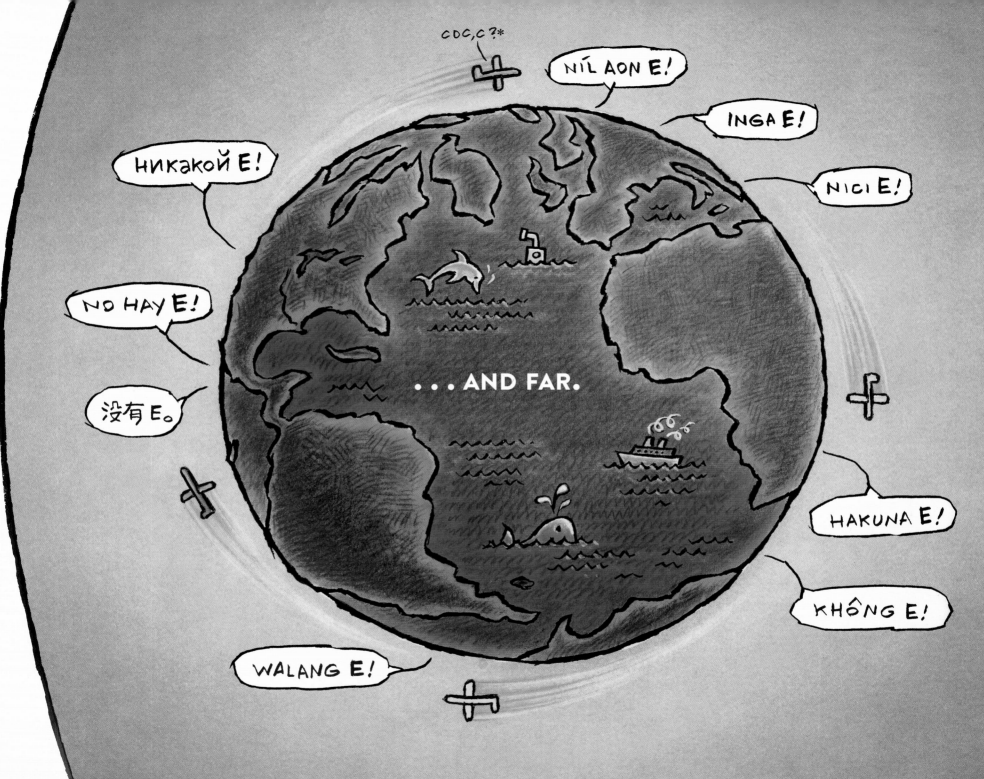

WHEN THEY GOT HOME, E STILL WASN'T RECOVERED.

THE LETTERS HAD A PROBLEM.

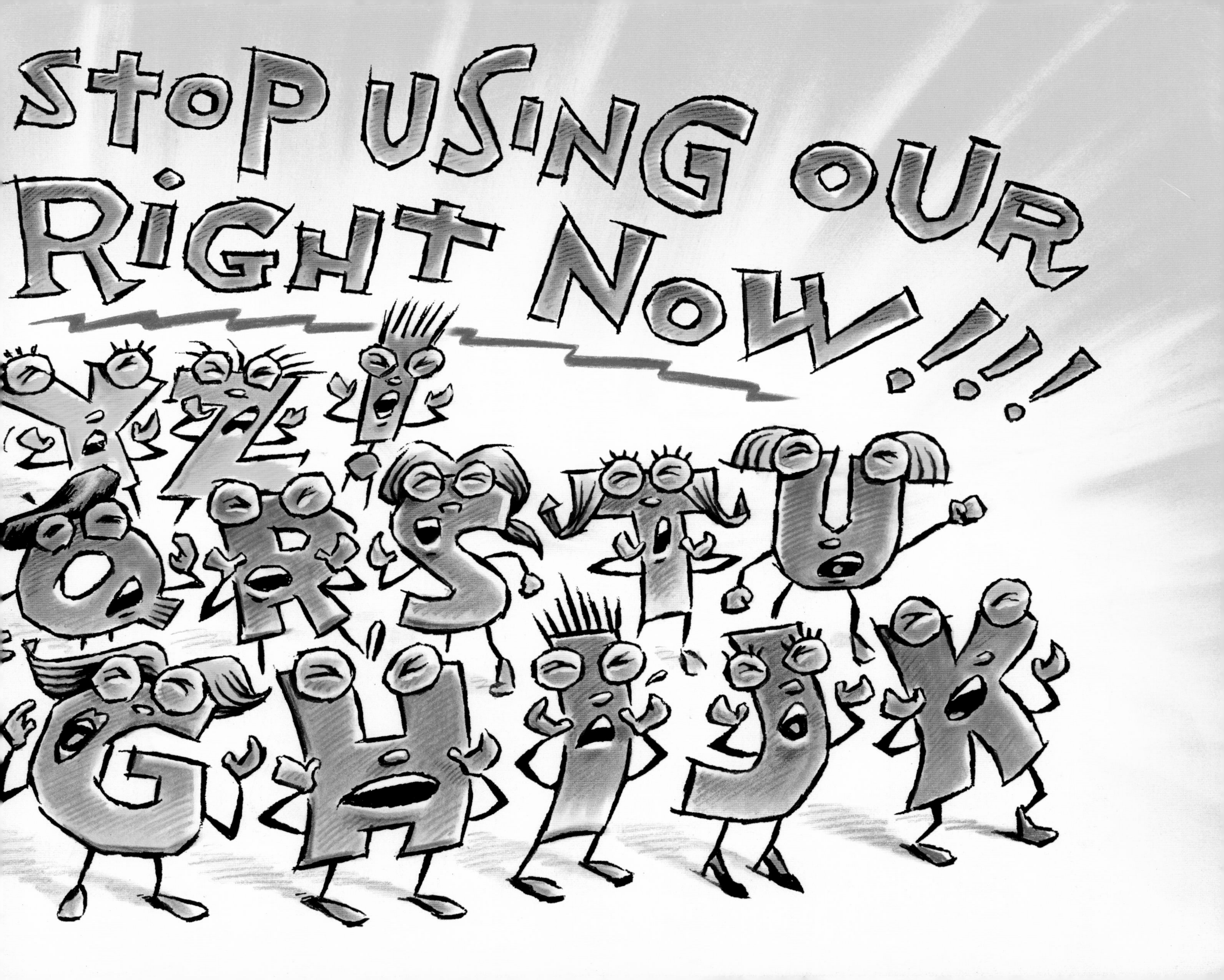
STOP USING OUR RIGHT NOW!!!

SO THO LAST PORSON USING YOU-KNOW-WHO STOPPOD.

QUICK AS A WINK, SHO WAS OUT OF BOD AND ROADY TO GO BACK TO WORK.

JUST IN TIMO FOR . . .

thE End.

F G Y P B V K J X Q Z

TOM LICHTENHELD loves drawing pictures and telling silly stories. His books include the *New York Times* **bestsellers** *Duck! Rabbit!*, *Goodnight, Goodnight, Construction Site*, **and** *Steam Train, Dream Train*. He lives in Geneva, Illinois.

EZRA FIELDS-MEYER is a high school student and an expert animator. He is the creator of the animated short "Alphabet House," which inspired this book, and is the subject of the memoir *Following Ezra* (by his father, Tom Fields-Meyer). He lives in Los Angeles.

For resources, visit www.chroniclebooks.com/classroom.